Finn's New Game

Story by Jill McDougall
Illustrations by Michael Emmerson

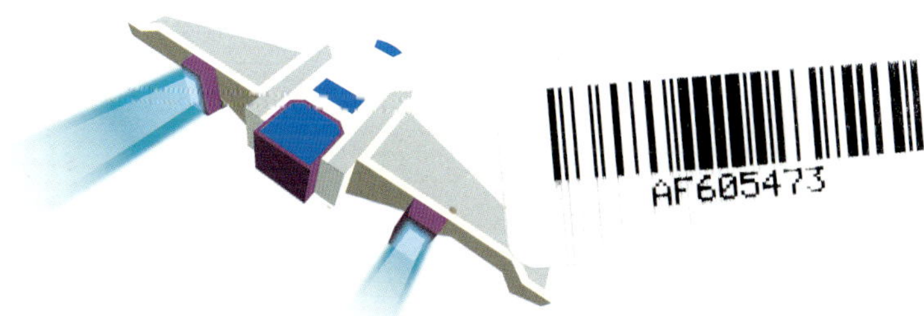

Contents

Chapter 1

A New Game

Finn was at school talking with his friend Ethan.

"Have you played *Comet Blaster*?" asked Ethan. "It's a new game on the internet and it's really good."

"How do you play it?" Finn asked.

Ethan looked excited. "You zoom around in a spaceship and zap comets," he said. "You win Star Points for every comet you hit."

"That sounds like fun!" said Finn. "I could play it on our laptop at home."

"You can talk to other people who are playing," said Ethan, smiling. "You might see my spaceship. It's called RocketMan3!"

After school, Finn raced inside to ask Mum if he could play *Comet Blaster*.

"Mum's still at work," said Finn's big sister, Lauren.

"Can I play a game on the laptop?" Finn asked her. "It's called *Comet Blaster*. My friend Ethan plays it."

"Okay," said Lauren. "As long as you're quiet. I have homework to do."

Finn quickly downloaded *Comet Blaster*.

Then, he made up a good name
for his spaceship: MoonWalker7.

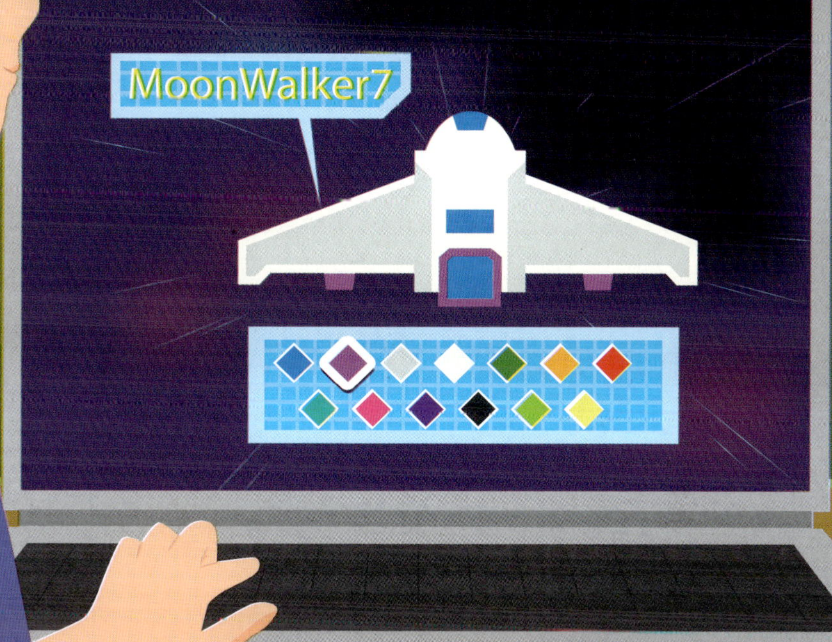
MoonWalker7

Chapter 2

StarShip9

Soon, Finn's spaceship was zooming past hundreds of stars.

A giant comet flew close by.

Quickly, Finn tapped the controls for his spaceship.
A ball of flame shot out from the front of his spaceship and melted the icy comet.

Now I have six Star Points, thought Finn.
This is fun!

Finn could see other spaceships.
He looked for one called RocketMan3,
but Ethan's spaceship was not there.

6

Suddenly, a little chat window popped up on Finn's screen.

Someone had sent him a message:

Hi MoonWalker7. You're a good player.

The message was from someone called StarShip9.

Finn felt proud. He sent a message back:

Thanks, StarShip9.

The window disappeared and Finn kept playing. He wanted to win more Star Points before Mum arrived home.

Chapter 3

A Strange Message

Suddenly, Finn's spaceship was in danger.
Space rocks were flying towards it!

Just then, another message appeared from StarShip9:

Hi MoonWalker7. I can show you how to get away from space rocks.

Finn answered back:

Thanks, StarShip9.

The next message from StarShip9 said:

But first you have to tell me your real name.

Finn stared at the message.
It made him feel funny in his tummy.

"That's not right!" Finn said to himself.

Quickly, Finn closed the game.

Chapter 4

Staying Safe

When Mum arrived home, Finn told her about the message from StarShip9.

"You did the right thing, Finn," said Mum.
"We don't know who StarShip9 is.
We will block them.
That means they can't send you messages any more."

Together, Mum and Finn blocked StarShip9.
"Can I still play *Comet Blaster*?" Finn asked.

Mum watched the spaceships on the screen for a moment.

"Yes, you can," said Mum, at last.
"But only play when I am home."
Mum patted Finn's arm gently.
"From now on, you must only talk to people you know," she said.

Chapter 5
RocketMan3

The next day after school,
Finn sat down to play *Comet Blaster*.

He flew his spaceship alongside a bright green comet.

Zap!

Finn tapped the controls and melted the comet
with a ball of flame.

13

Suddenly, a message popped up on Finn's screen.

It was from RocketMan3:

Hi Finn! I can help you get away from the black hole.

Quickly, Finn sent an answer:

Thanks, Ethan … I mean, RocketMan3!

Ethan's next message said:

Fly in a straight line towards my spaceship.

Before long, Finn's spaceship was safe.

Soon, he was zooming through space,
zapping the brightest comets he could find.
Zap! Zap! Zap!